Three by the Sea

MINI GREY

ALFRED A. KNOPF
New York

On a pebbly stretch of shore
in a beach hut by the sea,
there lived a black cat,
a white dog,
and a little
gray mouse.

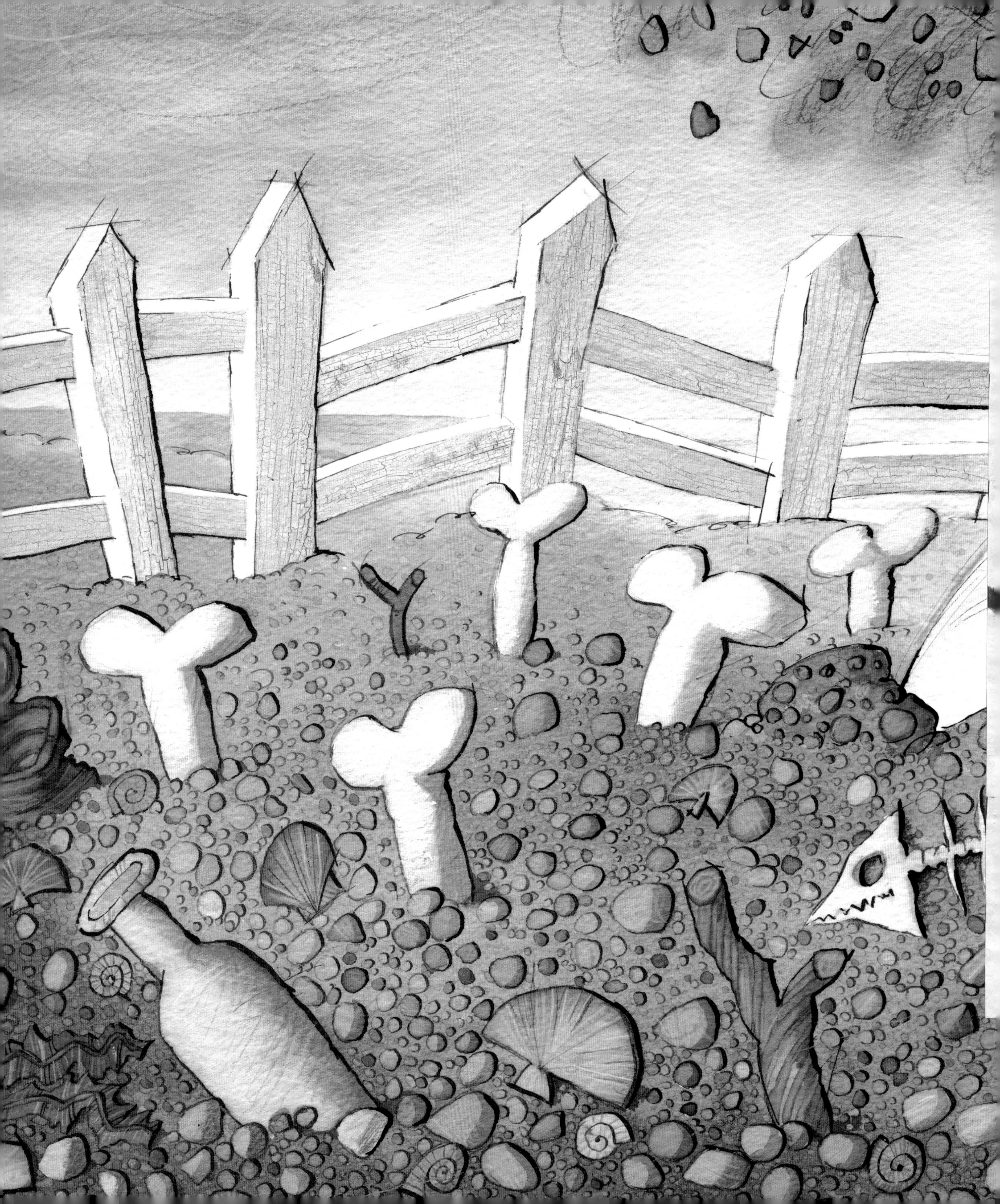

The dog tended
to the garden.

The cat took care of the housework.

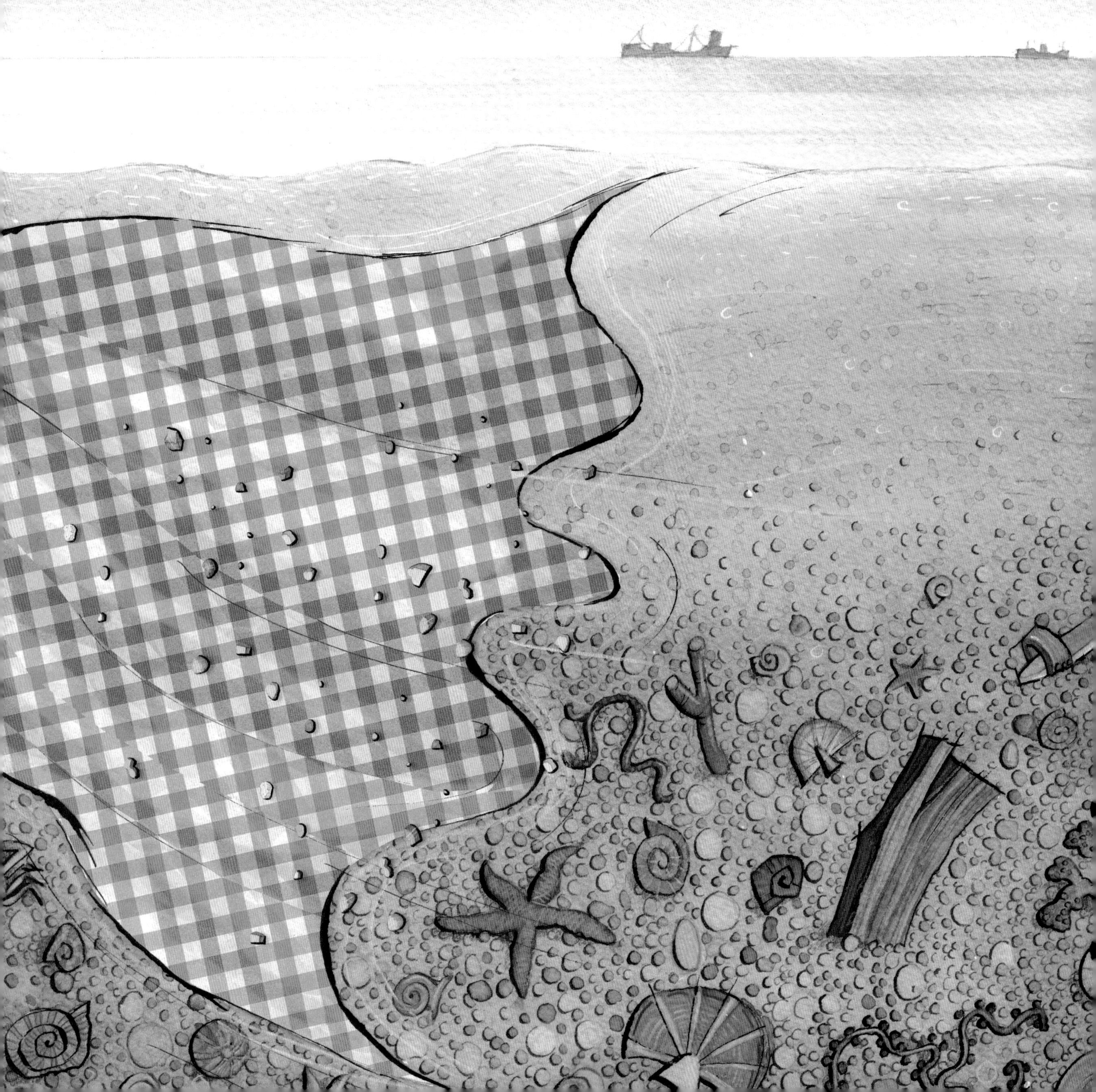

The mouse
looked after
the cooking.

And they lived happily.

Or so they thought.

1001 FAVOURITE FONDUES
HOT CHEESE FONDUE
You will need:
Gruyère Cheese
Emmenthal Cheese
Cheddar Cheese
and for decoration:
Parmesan Cheese
METHOD
Grate the cheeses a large cooking pot. on a gentle heat, stirring constantly until the cheeses are melted. On no account allow it to burn.
Decorate with shavings of Parmesan.
1001 FAVOURITE FONDUES
EXTRA CHEESY FONDUE
INGREDIENTS:
Roquefort Cheese
Gorgonzola Cheese
Stilton Cheese
Camembert Cheese
WHAT TO DO:
Keep the cheeses warm for several days until aromatic. Chop the cheeses finely and mix. Warm through in your fondue pot. Under no circumstances let your mixture boil quickly, otherwise it becomes tough and rubbery.
GOOD MOUSEKEEPING'S COOKERY COMPENDIUM
WAVERLEY
ALL-PURPOSE FLAKES
ALL-PURPOSE FLAKES
Perfect for:
breakfast
snacks
baking
bathing
washing
rinsing
scouring
AND MANY MORE USES
INGREDIENTS
BEER

One night
a Stranger blew in
to the shore

and found his way to
the beach hut by the sea.

He invited himself in.

The Stranger announced
that they were
the Lucky Winners
of a visit from the
WINDS OF CHANGE
TRADING COMPANY
and it would be
absolutely FREE.

He explained that if you felt
strangely discontented,
or wondered if your life
was missing
a special Something,
then ***WINDS OF CHANGE***
was the company for you.

And, of course,
everything was
ABSOLUTELY
FREE.

The Stranger also explained
that he needed to sleep
in a proper bed
with plenty of pillows
and eiderdowns.

There was only one bed.

The next day, after breakfast, the Stranger took Mouse aside and said: "You know, Mouse, I don't mean to be rude about Dog, but his idea of gardening is a bit odd.

He only plants bones!
Who wants a bone garden?
Where are the flowers?
Where are the vegetables?
Where are the herbs?"

The Stranger
gave Mouse
some things to read
from his suitcase.

After lunch the Stranger
said to Dog:
"Dog–while you've been busy
digging the garden,
Cat has been doing the housework.
Come and look at Cat
doing the housework."

"Hmmm," said Dog.
"Well, we didn't sleep very well
last night."

But he felt a little upset.

The Stranger
gave Dog
a present too.

Around suppertime the Stranger found Cat alone and said:

"You know, Cat, I've never been that keen on fondue myself–but I suppose that mice never get tired of cheese. Do you have fondue every night?"

"Pretty much," said Cat.

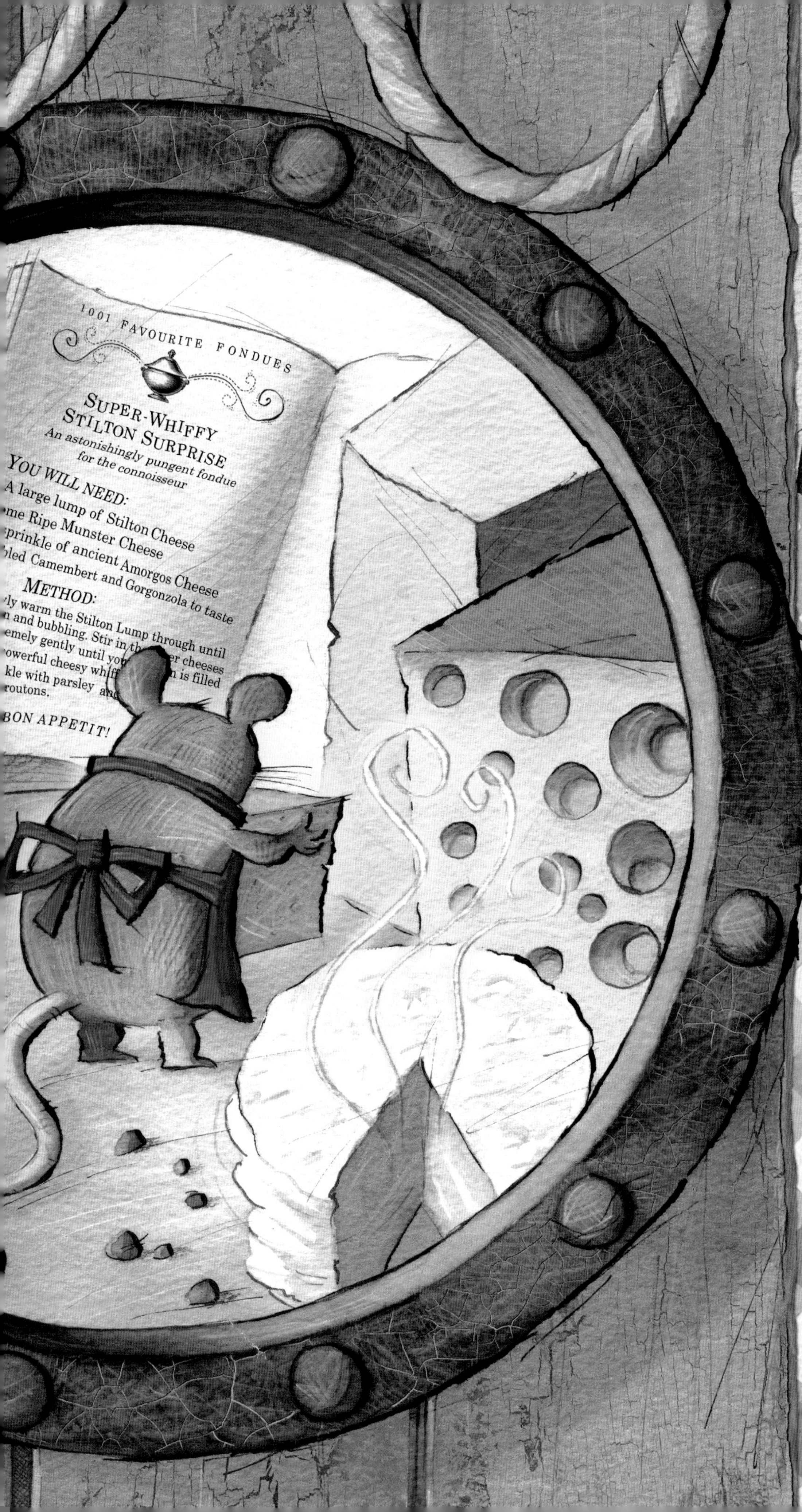
1001 FAVOURITE FONDUES
SUPER-WHIFFY STILTON SURPRISE
An astonishingly pungent fondue for the connoisseur
YOU WILL NEED:
A large lump of Stilton Cheese
me Ripe Munster Cheese
prinkle of ancient Amorgos Cheese
bled Camembert and Gorgonzola to taste
METHOD:
ly warm the Stilton Lump through until
n and bubbling. Stir in th er cheeses
emely gently until yo
owerful cheesy whiff n is filled
kle with parsley and
routons.
BON APPETIT!

CAT BRAND
SARDINES

Cat also got
some gifts
from the suitcase.

WINDS OF CHANGE FISHERIES LTD.
A Feast of Fresh Fish
MACKEREL
IN TOMATO SAUCE

At dinner
everyone was very quiet, until–
"A spot more fondue, anyone?"
asked Mouse,
and . . .

Why do we always have to have fondue?

Well, you do the cooking, then, if you don't like it.

Maybe I will.

Well, maybe you won't fall asleep while you're doing it.

What do you mean?

I saw you doing your so-called cleaning.

That's not fair, Dog.
What about the garden?
When did we say that we
wanted a bone garden?

Your cooking is horrible.

Your housework is rubbish.

Your garden's
a mess.

That night while Cat and Dog
were trying to sleep,

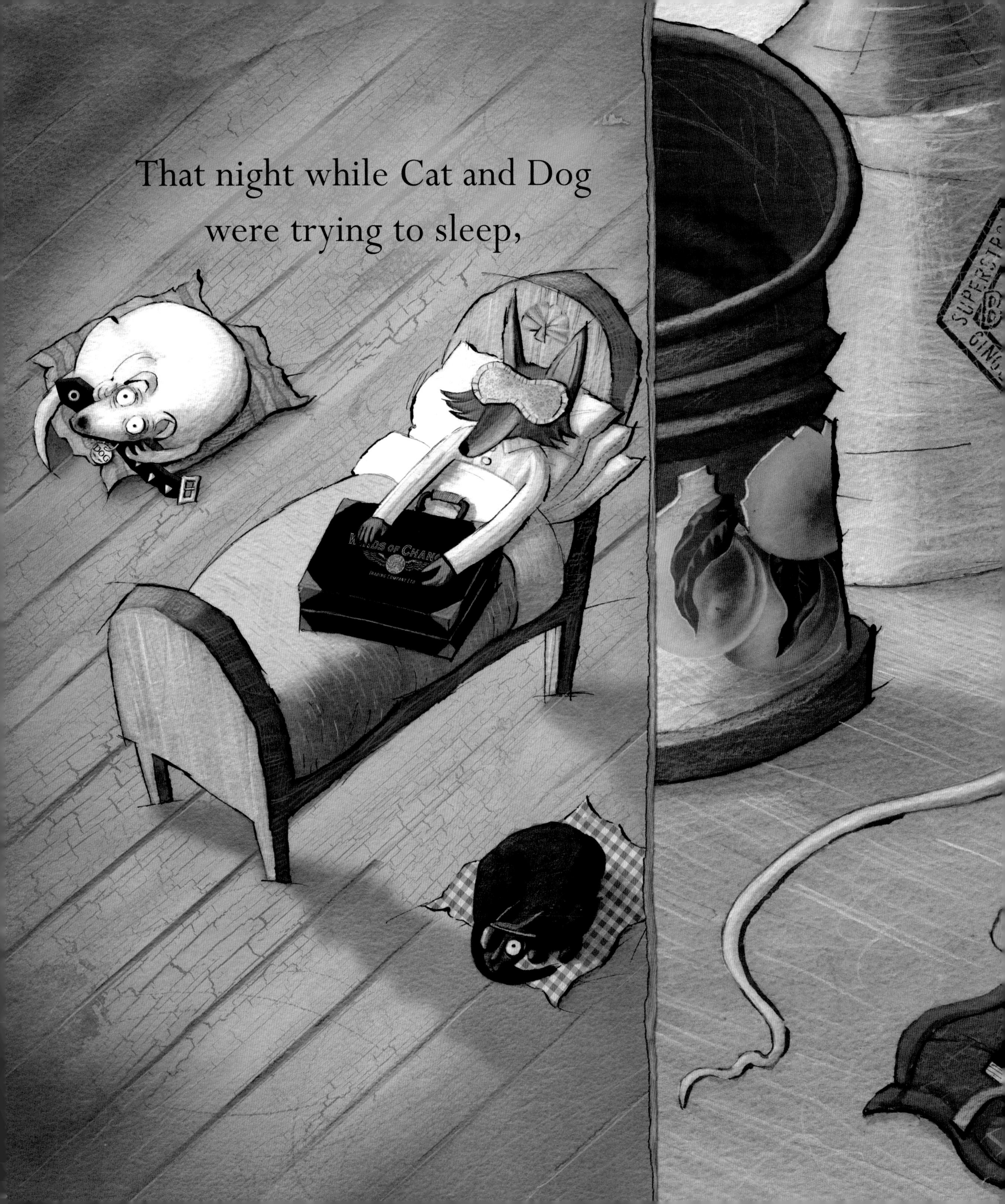

Mouse was
packing his things,
planning to travel
to somewhere
where his cooking
was appreciated.

At about midnight the cat woke
with a lurch and a sinking feeling
that something was wrong.

She walked
along the seafront.
On the pebbles was a bundle
of things–the sort of things
that belonged to Mouse.

Through
the roar
of the sea
her keen ears
heard a desperate
faraway squeak.

Cat couldn't swim,
but she waded
into the water anyway.

She just had to
rescue Mouse.

Cat scooped up Mouse
and put him on her head,
but she was having trouble
staying afloat.

Then, from
the watery darkness,
a pale blob got
nearer and nearer
and nearer.

Dog was a good swimmer,
good enough
for all three
of them.

Dog carried them all
to safety on the shore.

Back on the
beach
they made sure
that everyone
was still alive
and nobody
was drowned.

They all agreed
it was probably
time for
the Stranger
to leave.

But in the beach hut
there was not a shred
of the Stranger
or his suitcase.
Except a note,
and these packets
of seeds.

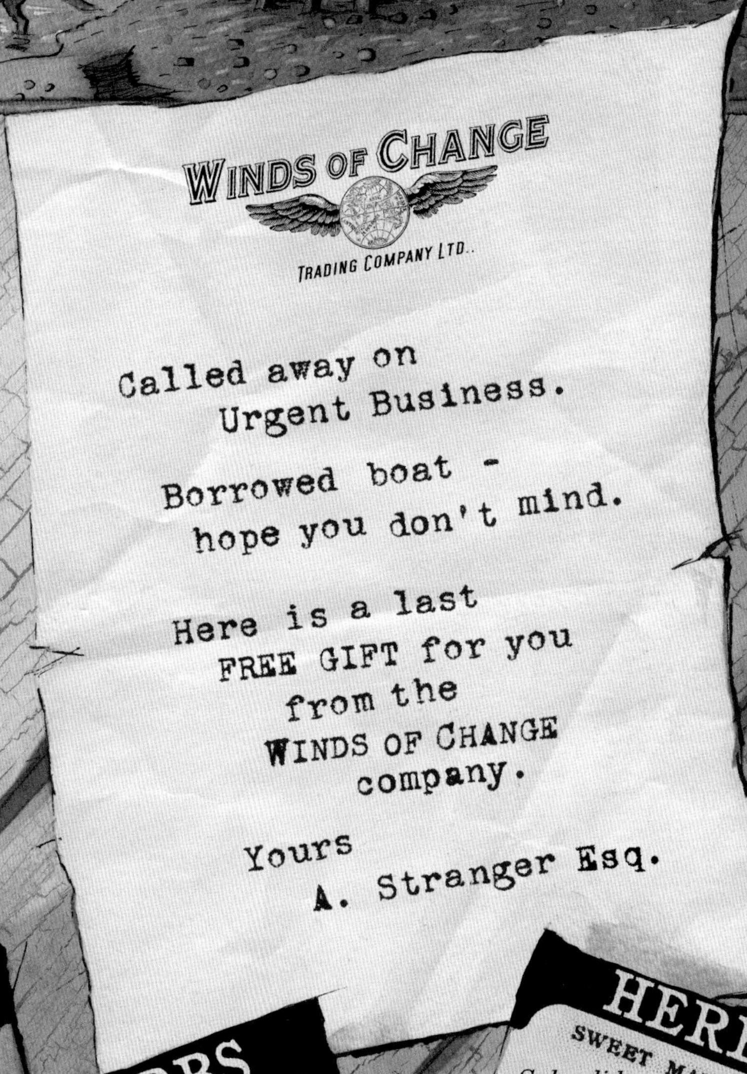

WINDS OF CHANGE
TRADING COMPANY LTD..

Called away on
Urgent Business.

Borrowed boat -
hope you don't mind.

Here is a last
FREE GIFT for you
from the
WINDS OF CHANGE
company.

Yours
A. Stranger Esq.

And now, if you happened to drop by
the beach hut near the sea,
you might notice that they
were doing things
a little differently.

You might see
Mouse and Dog
cultivating their
bone and herb garden.

Or you might see
Cat and Mouse making
cheese and sardine fondue
(with a twist of thyme and a bay leaf).

If it was first thing
in the morning,
you'd most probably hear
Cat and Dog humming a tune
as they kept the hut
cozy and clean.

And you just
might notice
a scent of herbs
in the sea air.

FOR OUR OWN HERB

THIS IS A BORZOI BOOK PUBLISHED BY ALFRED A. KNOPF

 Published in the United States by Alfred A. Knopf,
an imprint of Random House Children's Books, a division of Random House, Inc., New York.
Originally published in hardcover in Great Britain by Jonathan Cape,
an imprint of Random House Children's Books,
a division of the Random House Group Limited, London, in 2010.

Library of Congress Cataloging-in-Publication Data is available upon request.
ISBN 978-0-375-86784-2 (trade) — ISBN 978-0-375-96784-9 (lib. bdg.)

MANUFACTURED IN CHINA
April 2011
10 9 8 7 6 5 4 3 2 1

First American Edition

SPECIAL THANKS TO THE BRAINPOWER OF ANDREA